WINDMOLEN

The Secret of
The Windmill by the Bay

Simon Finn

Illustrated by Simon Goodway

Illustrated by Simon Goodway.

Image of *At the Seaside* used with permission of the Metropolitan Museum of Art, New York, NY, U.S.A. Chase, William Merritt (1849–1916). Ca 1892. Oil on Canvas, 20 x 34 in. (50.8 x 86.4 cm). Bequest of Miss Adelaide Milton de Groot (1876–1967), 1967 (67.187.123). Image copyright © The Metropolitan Museum of Art/Art Resource, NY.

Cover photographs by Simon Finn.

Find the clues...

The title of the next book in this series is hidden in this story. Perhaps you can spot the pattern and find the answer?

Please visit WindmillByTheBay.com for more information.

To Elaine

No one can tell me,
Nobody knows,
Where the wind comes from,
Where the wind goes.

A. A. Milne, "Wind on the Hill" (1927)

Contents

Part I

Part II

Part One

⌘

Chapter One

The Cannonball from Hunterspoint

Every now and then I find myself remembering the time I got caught up in what you might call a real adventure. For a second, I'll wonder if I imagined the whole thing. It sometimes seems too impossible that it would have all worked out just the way it did, and I'll doubt myself. Friends tell me I am sort of a daydreamer, someone who likes to watch the passing clouds and who thinks he sees the shapes of people or rabbits or some such things in a drifting pattern in the sky, but this adventure did happen. I'm sure of that.

Little things will bring me back to that time and revive memories of every detail; even the sound of a train can trigger them. I think that's because it all started with a trip on the Long Island Rail Road to the town of Westhampton. It could also be because the sound of a train's horn is almost part of the landscape out on the East End of Long Island, and that's where this story unfolded.

It began one summer when George—he likes to be called Geo—phoned me on a Friday at my office in Manhattan. I was a little surprised but always welcomed hearing from him and perhaps finding an excuse to head out to the beach. I could see the weather would improve a little before becoming stormy again.

I work as a meteorologist for a TV station in New York City and so, of course, am very aware of the weather patterns. I could see that the barometer was rising as the bad conditions we had been experiencing would improve slightly—for a little while anyway. Nothing like trading the green glow of the weather-tracking computer screens for the prospect of at least brighter skies. Not a bad time to visit Geo by the beach. Besides, I was about to take off a few days from work anyway.

"Paul, come right away," he said. "I have a mystery to solve, and I'll need your help." He went on to describe the discovery of a drawing—some sort of map, but it wasn't clear why I needed to hurry.

"I have no plans this weekend and can take the *Cannonball* express from Hunterspoint," I explained. "What's the rush? If this is a treasure map, won't the treasure wait?"

"I am not sure it is a treasure map," said Geo. "But I think this document points to a secret of some sort. We need to figure a few things out. I am not sure what we have here." Geo was quiet for a moment and added, "I'll pick you up in

Westhampton." He doesn't always explain everything clearly. He thinks very quickly and doesn't slow down to express all his thoughts.

As you might imagine, my mind was racing as I made my way to the train, the 4:06 p.m. Long Island Rail Road departure from Hunterspoint, which is nicknamed the *Cannonball*. I stopped briefly at my apartment to pack some clothes and things. I even grabbed a book I had been reading for the train ride. It's funny that as I quickly packed to head off on this adventure I thought of someone who would play a role in this story—the "pirate" Captain Kidd. Why did I think of him? Well, he has always been a bit of a mystery. Here was a man living comfortably in lower Manhattan. He was well connected and by most measures successful. He had a wife and children and even owned some docks not too far from where I was living on the Upper East Side, and he left it all. He set off on the high seas and fought like a pirate. He was eventually put to death in London after being accused of being a pirate. Now, how did he go from a comfortable life in New York to being hanged for piracy? Well, let's leave that for later.

I have to say I was not someone looking to skip out on my job, not exactly, but from time to time I did feel a need to get away from the usual routine. Don't get me wrong. I love analyzing the weather patterns and trying to predict how they will develop. It's an important job since weather affects almost every activity in some way: flights get delayed because of the weather, schools close in the winter because of snow, and base-ball games get rained out. Everyone wants to know the weather for the next day. I never tire of my job. But I do tire of people who are uncomfortable living with ambiguity and the unknown. Not knowing the future precisely is a big part of my job as a meteorologist.

The weather is a lot like life. You can observe the patterns and have an idea of what is coming next, but you never know for sure. Too many unknown factors interact with each other in too many complex ways to calculate with one hundred percent certainty what will happen next. Folks like me who predict the weather warn people when it looks like a storm is coming, but sometimes it does not develop as we had thought. Our success is in helping people prepare by narrowing the range of possibilities. Wouldn't you rather know there is a good chance it will rain the day you are planning a picnic than to have no idea it could happen?

Almost every day people will call the studio where I work, e-mail me, or stop me on the subway and do one of two things: they either blame me for recent stormy weather, as if I create the weather patterns, or they get impatient with me because I never tell them exactly how the weather will be for the next day. It gets tiring. Years ago I tried more often to tell them what a miracle it is that modern computers, smart sensors all over the country, and years of experience allow us to predict a range of likely weather patterns, but I don't think most people understand.

So, I have adopted a variety of coping responses. Sometimes I just laugh along with them when they thank me for the blue skies or blame me for the rain. I tell them that if they are really good to me, I will make sure more good weather comes. Or I joke that we meteorologists really know the weather in detail for decades into the future because of our magic computers but that we like to keep some mystery in the air so that we don't lose our jobs. I use my best confessional voice to whisper to them that we just like the attention and want folks to watch us on TV every day, so we make it seem more mysterious than it is, but that is not at all the case. It's a hard job because there are so many variables.

Like I said, some folks are just not comfortable accepting that you cannot know the future for sure. That's the way the weather is. That's the way life is. And probably one of the most difficult things to understand, far more difficult than understanding the weather, is understanding people and why they make the choices they do. People have secrets. They also sometimes do things for reasons they themselves do not understand.

Anyway, I made my way to the subway and would link up with the Long Island Rail Road. There was no way I could concentrate on the book I had packed once I was seated on the train. Instead, I kept trying to figure out what kind of exciting search I had embarked on, but without more information, my thoughts were just spinning in circles. At one point I had the bright idea of doing an Internet search from my cell phone for anything about the Hamptons and a map. I got nowhere fast. Just lots of Internet pages of maps of the Hamptons. I was getting restless sitting on the train with its rows of silent passengers who barely even looked at each other but who, ironically, seemed very concerned with their appearance.

I was very relieved when the train reached Westhampton about a quarter to six. Just the smell of the air as I got off the train told me I had left the city far behind. There was a salty freshness that I always forget about until the next time I step off the train from the city and arrive near the beach. Decades ago the smell of salt in the air was accompanied by the earthy scent of potato farms and the distinctively charming aroma of large duck farms. But many of the old potato fields are now residential neighborhoods, and I cannot remember the last time I passed a duck farm.

It wasn't hard to find Geo. His car always looked a little different from all the others, and he always parked in a spot away from the crowd, ready to take off ahead of the rest of the vehicles that came down to pick up friends and family getting off the train, even when he was not in a rush. Geo was always thinking ahead like that.

This time, it was especially easy to find him. His car was all polished and painted a dark shade of blue. It appeared like no other. Sure, it had four wheels and four doors and everything else that looked normal. It also had, however, the curvy lines of something more like a car from the 1950s, or even of a boat.

I've known Geo for years. He lives out on Long Island's East End in an area called Shinnecock Hills. Shinnecock is the name of a local Native American community, and it lends its name to the area. I used to spend the summers out that way, and Geo was one of our neighbors.

He lives alone in a big stone house right on the beach. It's the color of sand and almost looks like a castle of sorts—a sand castle, you could say. The house is made up of geometric stone shapes stacked on each other, but there aren't any towers, and there is no moat. Nothing like that. And it has plenty of windows—not a dark place at all. In front of the house, a pier runs from the beach right into the water. The dock always smells of creosote and low tide. A green light on a little lamppost at the end of the dock is like a little beacon for those cruising at night to find their way.

Geo lives in his sand castle house and also has several other buildings on his property to store all his "projects." He's an electrical engineer who retired after making a fortune on some sort of clever but obscure invention. He's always rewiring appliances to make them work better and has at least one and a half, perhaps one and three-quarters, cars in his garage. This might seem to be a strange way to count something as big as a car, but the way he rebuilds and redesigns his car—cars?—makes it hard to keep track. And there are always parts everywhere, even after he says he has finished a project. It looks like a mess, but he knows his way around the piles.

9

Geo is about sixty years old. His dark hair is graying here and there, and his tanned and creased face is more like that of a farmer than someone who has spent lots of time bent over his workbench fixing electrical widgets. He never talks much about his family. This might be because of his very practical approach—always focused on the logical and the rational. His positive personality comes through most clearly in the way he always thinks things can be improved through reason and his tendency to make detailed plans to make the improvements happen. Now I had another chance to work with him on one of his projects.

He never waited on the train platform for anyone. Not only because he wanted to beat the crowds by waiting in the car but because he sometimes has trouble walking. Geo used a cane occasionally to help him walk. There is some story—the details of which have never been made entirely clear to me—about a leg injury and a helicopter flight decades ago. He rarely said much whenever the topic came up. I wondered if that was why he was looking for my help with this "mystery," as he called it, because if there is anyone who needs less help figuring anything out it is Geo. This added to the surprise of his request to come join him right away. He usually carried out all his "projects" by himself, seeing other people as in the way.

"Glad you could make it," he said as I got up to the car. "You must be wondering why I dragged you out this way."

Geo has always had a sense for what people are thinking. He has told me countless times that you can almost "hear" what a person is thinking from a block away by the look on his or her face or from the way he or she walks. He probably didn't even need to see me to expect this question after what he had told me on the phone.

"You spent lots of time out this way in your younger days," he said. "Together we can try to figure out this mystery I have stumbled into. The clues we have so far seem to refer to places and perhaps people from the area. You bring special knowledge. Get in the car and let me tell you more as we drive to my house."

I was happy to be away from the city and glad to finally have a chance to learn more about the clues. I couldn't wait to see the map-like drawing he had mentioned on the phone. It was a document that definitely pointed to something—but what?

Chapter Two

The Dog on the Beach
And the Map in the Box

We sat around the table in Geo's living room, which looked right out on Great Peconic Bay in front of his house. Not that we could really see the bay with all the fog. The sky, fog, and the bay all ran together not far off shore, as if someone had not drawn them in yet. It made us feel as though we were floating in boundless clouds or hemmed in by a great wall of nothingness at the same time.

I had him repeat for me how he found the rumpled map we now had in front of us. He explained again, "As I don't need to tell you, we have had some stormy days. Last night the wind blew hard, and waves were pounding. It quieted down by morning, but it seemed colder than is normal for August." Geo pointed to where the storm had obviously churned up the beach. The strong winds must have added energy to the waves, which often get quite large when the weather turns for the worse. He continued, "To add to it, there was a dog digging on the beach right over there. It was a bear-like dog. Any time I approached, he would look right at me with his big face. There was no chance I was going to move closer."

I knew that these were not good omens for Geo. He paid close attention to the weather and probably found the conditions this morning particularly unsettled. To top it all off, he was afraid of dogs. This sounded like a big one. All the dog had to do was to look at him, and Geo would be scared off.

Geo continued his story, "When I finally went down to the shoreline at low tide, long after the dog had gone, I saw that heaps of sand had been kicked up and something was sticking out. It was this wooden box with a metal lock." He pointed to the old box on the floor. It was about the size of a laptop but many times thicker. Near it were the metal pieces of the lock that he had sliced with special cutters. "Inside the box was a bottle with a cork in it. And inside the bottle was this drawing."

The map looked old stretched out on the table. I could make out shapes that seemed to represent land and water, but the most remarkable aspect of the document was all the odd symbols, words, letters, and drawings that were handwritten in various locations across its surface. It immediately made me think of a treasure map.

"Some people might look at this and think they have a treasure map," said Geo, as if he was reading my mind.

"Well, it does look pretty old, and it seems to be a mysterious map pointing to something," I said cautiously, knowing already that he seemed to think the idea of treasure was silly.

"Let's line up what we know, and see what we can figure out," he said. "First, there has never been an actual case of any pirate, or anyone really, making a map that leads to some sort of treasure. Never."

"Not once?" I asked.

"Not once. This would be the first, if that's what it is."

"Well, where do we get all the stories about pirates and treasure maps, AND," I added with a sense of triumph, "the big X on a map to show where a treasure is located? Everyone knows that's how it's done! X marks the spot! The big X!"

"Those are just old stories," said Geo. "Authors like Robert Lewis Stevenson came up with tales...fun tales, sure...but made-up tales, just fiction, about pirates. Those old stories don't help us much here, at least not as far as I can tell."

The "map" seemed to show land and water, but scattered around the document were strange pictures. There was a violin, and a sailboat, and an umbrella—two umbrellas, actually. There was also a drawing of what looked like a seal or otter of some sort. In one place was the word "dinosaurs." In another, "xjtdpotjo" was neatly written. What looked like the letter M was written in another spot. Finally, there was the word "groot." Quite a collection of little doodles and odd words, but I could not make any sense out of them. The shapes of what might

15

have been water and land did not even seem to correspond to the geography of this area, but the curious map seemed to be the key to understanding something.

"What do you think?" Geo said.

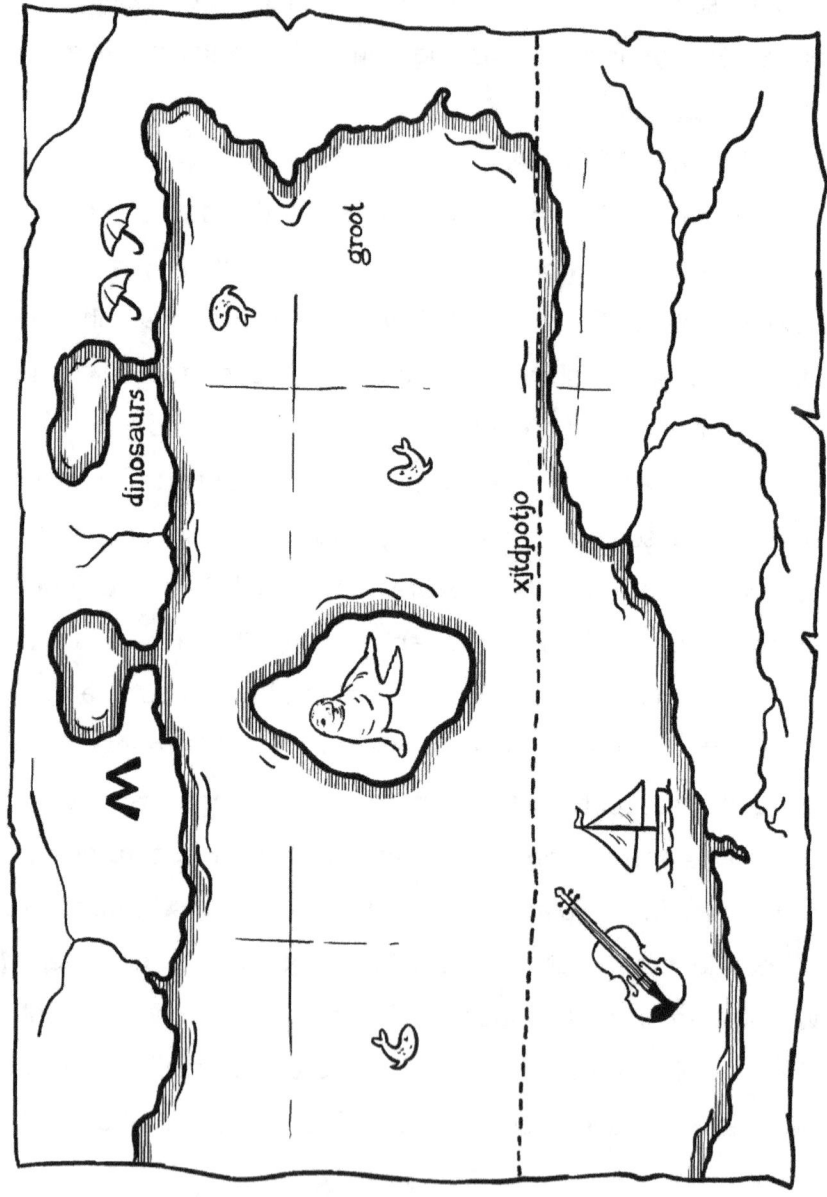

"Well, let me look now at the bottle you found this map in and the box as well." I picked up the bottle. It was a little grimy but was in good shape and made of clear glass with no markings. The box looked as though it had been in the water. The lock was dirty and sandy but bright and shiny when you brushed it off. "I am not sure what to make of it," I said quietly.

"How old would you say this stuff is?" he asked, as if he already had an idea.

"Hmm...that map looks old to me."

"Old? Or just well used and worn? As if it has been folded a lot and perhaps exposed to sun and salt water?" Geo asked looking closely and expectantly for my reaction, as if he was trying to plant some seeds in my thinking.

"It's hard for me to tell. It looks as though it definitely has been folded or rolled up quite a bit."

"I don't think that paper is more than thirty years old or so," Geo said confidently. He held it up to the light. "Look at the watermark."

I held the paper up to the light. There was the outline of what looked like a little recycling symbol.

"Did you know that the symbol was created by a college student who won a contest? Back in 1970?" Geo asked.

"No. So, this paper is not at all from the time of pirates or anything like that, is it? While we are talking about it, didn't Captain Kidd, the infamous pirate, sail around this area? When was he active?"

"There is a story that Captain Kidd buried treasure on Gardiners Island, east of here in Gardiners Bay. It was later dug up and turned over to officials for Captain Kidd's trial, but that was in the late 1600s, over three hundred years ago."

I remembered hearing about that story when I was a child. It always sparked my imagination to think that Captain Kidd actually sailed in the waters of the East End of Long Island. I had heard about the treasure being dug up on Gardiners Island, but, like many people, I liked to imagine that he buried other treasure out this way. I enjoyed thinking that there could be another place—perhaps several other spots—where he buried jewels and coins and gold. Why bury it all in one place? Divide it up and bury it in several locations for safekeeping, right?

Of course, I appreciated that Geo wanted to follow the evidence rationally, but what is the harm of dreaming a little, I thought to myself. "If anyone had secrets, it was Captain Kidd. If there was anyone who knew how to work around most people's expectations, it would have been Kidd!" I explained to Geo.

Kidd had left behind his family and business in Manhattan in the late 1600s to seek bigger fortunes as a privateer on behalf of England. A privateer was a sailor who had the permission of his government to attack ships of enemy countries. Kidd had done work like that before settling in New York and, therefore, knew how to do it well. He even managed to secure the backing of the King of England for his return to the high seas, but something happened along the way. According to some accounts, he started attacking almost any ship, not just the enemies of England, and went from being a privateer to a pirate, engaged in nasty and illegal activity.

He had planned to return to New York and resume his life as a regular member of society after making a fortune as a privateer, but word had spread that he had acted like a pirate. Instead of returning directly to New York City, he cautiously sailed around Long Island and tried to negotiate with the English officials in New York and Boston to avoid being arrested as a pirate. It is believed he buried many valuable items for retrieval later as he sailed around Long Island and negotiated.

"Another thing," Geo snapped me out of my daydream, "did you notice the lock? Dirty, but not rusty. And that box would never last long in the salt water."

"So it is a modern map that has not been buried long?"

"It is at least a map designed to record a secret, but I think it was very quickly stashed in that bottle with the cork that does not exactly match and placed in that wooden box, which is not designed to last long in salt water. I think someone was keeping track of something he or she wanted to keep secret on this paper—what we are calling a 'map.' It seems to me the author of the map might have found a location of something valuable and, in a hurry, had to get rid of this map. Perhaps they hoped it would lead others to...I'm not sure what to."

It did not seem like much to go on. He was always a very practical person and almost always right or at least mostly right. We worked late into the evening trying to see if we could make progress by searching on the Internet. It was a long night with little to show for it.

Chapter Three

Developing New Leads at the Rogers Memorial Library

"Why don't we go to the police?" I asked as we drove into Southampton the next morning.

"We have no choice," Geo answered. "We go to the police, and they will laugh at us with so little evidence. They will have to take care of more pressing matters. They cannot spend time chasing this down, but I believe there is something here. Let's hold onto the clues, and we can always go to the police and turn this stuff in after we have checked all that we can." In my experience Geo has a strong track record of having his hunches turn into something significant. I was ready to work with him on this.

And so we drove into Southampton, which, because it was summer, was busy with usual summer activity. There were nannies taking someone else's children to tennis lessons or the

21

beach; contractors making their rounds maintaining other people's lawns, pools, and hedges; and countless weekend and
summer residents who left the now empty Manhattan behind to
join the throngs getting away from it all and quickly discovering
it all followed them. Some short-term visitors were so busy trying to figure out where they could stop without getting a parking ticket, they wondered if the reportedly beautiful beaches
were really just a myth whose secret was maintained by inac-
cessible parking areas open only to residents holding fabled
window stickers.

We parked next to the Rogers Memorial Library, a large,
relatively new building whose warm shingles and classic lines
hide a modern facility. I find it a pleasure to go there. And
that's saying a lot for me, as I have had mixed feelings about
libraries over the years. At their worst, they manage to com-
bine an industrial and cold architectural design, books that
aren't useful and probably weren't when they were first pub-
lished decades ago, along with a disturbing staff and even
stranger patrons who all roam about like zombies or those in
need of counseling who took a wrong turn and ended up in
the improper building. At their best, they have a capable staff,
are well stocked and pleasant to be in. Even more importantly
they offer two magic qualities that a good library can offer and
that the Internet can never replace: the magic of browsing for
material you did not realize you should be looking for and a
certain smell—not of mustiness—but the smell of the wisdom.

All right, perhaps that's just my perception. But the Rogers Memorial Library provides both, and we experienced both that day.

We headed inside. The cool air contrasted with the developing heat outside, and the humid air gave way to the magical smell of books. We made our way downstairs to the special room called the "Long Island Collection." It had just the sort of material that would likely help us: old maps, old photos, and books on the history of the area. Geo decided to look at the maps, nothing like what you can find online, to see if they offered clues. He also wanted to see if browsing some of the old books on the area would help us figure out any of the symbols on the map that he found on the beach. The library had just opened, and there were very few people there. It was a bit strange because we were not sure what we were looking for and did not want to advertise this map until we had a better idea of what it all meant.

There was no one else in the Long Island Collection room when we arrived. This gave us freedom to browse without worrying too much about other folks taking too much notice of what we were doing.

Our search the night before on the Internet yielded perhaps one helpful piece of information: the word "groot" on the map could mean "great" in Dutch. Why was this written in Dutch? And was this what the map's author intended? Or did the word "groot" have some other meaning for him or her? We

didn't know. We were just looking to move ahead in our investigation, sketching out the possibilities.

Before the English colonists controlled what is
now the New York area, the Dutch had significant influence. New York City had been called "New Amsterdam."
Henry Hudson sailed into what is now New York Harbor
in 1609 on behalf of the Dutch East India Company. In
1625, the Dutch believed they paid local Native Americans
for Manhattan Island. By 1664, the English had taken over
New Netherland, the colony the Dutch were creating on the
East Coast and that spanned from what is New York State
today into Connecticut and included parts of New Jersey,
Pennsylvania, and Delaware. There are still some Dutch
place names on Long Island that date from that time—like
"Lange Eylant" (Long Island) or "Breuckelen" (Brooklyn).
But from what we could tell in our Internet search, the
Dutch did not leave as much of a mark this far east on Long
Island. It seems that they stayed in the western part of
Long Island. *Who knows how this knowledge might help us
later in our search?* we thought to ourselves.

After about half an hour of browsing and brainstorming,
we found that we were not making much headway. I thought
I would ask a question of one of the librarians who had been
stacking and rearranging books for about fifteen minutes in the
special room we were in. She had long, dark hair and wore an
orange short-sleeved shirt and shorts, making her look like she

would be more comfortable in the summer sun than the well air-conditioned library.

Geo and I had agreed we would be cautious. We intentionally did not bring the map with us. We agreed we would ask vague questions and would not mention anything about finding a map. "Excuse me," I said. "Do you have any books that give a general outline of the influence of the Dutch on the East End of Long Island?"

"Hmm...," she thought hard. "What are you trying to research? The more you can tell me, the more I might be able to help you."

Geo stepped forward between the librarian and me. "We are helping a relative with a school project and thought we would begin with a basic outline. Nothing too complicated," he said.

"Is this school project about Dutch influence on Long Island? Or something more broad? Do you have anything more specific in mind?" she asked.

"Just a basic history book will do," said Geo quickly.

"It would be better if you told me more. Why did you pick this topic?" she asked.

"Personal interest," said Geo.

"I will see what I can do," she responded abruptly and left the room.

"That was very strange," wondered Geo out loud. "Most librarians usually offer a whole variety of options right off the top of their heads. She seemed so hesitant and defensive. Did you notice she folded her arms in front of her as she asked us what we were researching?"

"Is that important?" I asked.

"Well, it is odd, not a gesture that suggests she is open and welcoming at all, and why did she wait so long to offer to help us?"

Just then a man entered the room. He wore a sweater, perhaps to help him deal with the air-conditioned temperatures of the library. He looked at us very seriously and asked, "Can I help you gentlemen? I am sorry I did not even see you enter the Long Island Collection. We usually ask that you leave bags like that knapsack you are carrying, at the front desk before coming in here. That's to prevent anyone from leaving with the valuable documents we have here. I guess you stepped in here right when we opened, and I missed you." He pointed to my small, black bag.

"That's strange—your colleague did not say anything," Geo replied.

"My colleague?" questioned the librarian.

"Yes, the young lady who was just helping us," I answered.

The librarian looked very surprised. "I think there is some misunderstanding. The only other librarian on duty until two o'clock is Mrs. King. She would be very happy to hear that you refer to her as 'young.' She turned sixty-six years old last month, but I really don't think she could have been helping you anyway because we have been working side-by-side for the past hour sorting through some returned books and helping people at the front desk. Was this person you mentioned just in here recently?"

"About a minute before you stepped in the door," answered Geo.

"Was she wearing an orange shirt and shorts?'"

"Yes."

"I can tell you this much: she does not work here, but we have been looking for her. She came right to the front desk and kept Mrs. King and me very busy trying to help her with a list of very obscure requests. We finally located most of what she was looking for but found she had walked off without leaving her name. What did she say to you?" asked the librarian.

"We thought she worked here. And, frankly, also acted as if she did," I told the now bewildered man. "As a matter of fact, she just went off as if she was going to help us find a basic history of Dutch influence on Long Island."

"How strange," the librarian stammered. "Did you see her take anything from this room?'"

"No. She didn't carry anything," Geo told him.

"Well, let me tell Mrs. King about this. Something odd is going on. I will be right back to help you both. Let me check your bag at the front desk. I will be right back." He took my bag and left.

"How weird is that?" I exclaimed. "Why would someone pretend to be a librarian?"

"She was up to something. I thought it was strange that a librarian who works inside an air-conditioned building all day would be dressed for the heat outside. You might have noticed the real librarian wore a sweater because he works all day in this cool environment. I had my doubts about her."

"You had your doubts? Why did you let me ask her about our mystery? And who was she?"

"I don't know who she was, but she was watching us and wanted to find out more."

Just then the real librarian returned; this time he introduced himself as Jesse. "You gentlemen wanted books on the Dutch influence on Long Island, right? Well, there are a variety of sources—"

"Actually..." interrupted Geo. "I need to ask you this first. What can you tell me about this photo?" Geo walked us over to a display case that had a black-and-white photograph of a happy-looking man strolling outside with some children and with a huge umbrella on his shoulder.

"That's William Merritt Chase," said Jesse excitedly, "the American painter from the 1800s. And he's carrying a Japanese umbrella. Notice the cranes painted on the umbrella's surface."

I looked on with interest but was not sure how these facts were tied into the mystery we were trying to solve. The map had two umbrellas on it. But what was Geo expecting to find?

"Take a look here," said Jesse. He flipped through a big coffee table book with images of paintings. He opened the book to a page and placed the giant tome on the top of the display case with triumph. There on one page was a very large reproduction of a painting. It showed people in nineteenth-century clothes at the beach, and they were sitting under two huge umbrellas, just like the one William Merritt Chase was carrying in the photo, but there was a big difference: unlike the drabness of the black-and-white photo, the painting showed the Japanese umbrellas in brilliant colors: one was red and the other yellow.[1] "This painting was created in the 1890s. You can just make out the shapes of birds—cranes, actually—in this impressionistic painting. This was probably painted near Shinnecock Bay or Peconic Bay. Chase ran a summer art school out this way, and you can recognize parts of this area in the paintings. He is an important American artist."

"Do you have any books on William Merritt Chase that include an image of this painting and that we can check out? That would be very helpful," said Geo.

"Absolutely," said Jesse.

"And do you know if Chase played the violin or sailed?"

"I don't believe he did," Jesse answered. "Albert Einstein was known more for the violin, right? But I don't know about Chase. It's funny. You could say that Einstein was known for sailing, too. He sailed when he stayed out here on Long Island,

---

1   You will find an image of this painting, *At the Seaside*, on the back cover of this book.

but he was known for getting confused sometimes while in the boat."

"What's that?" Geo asked in a serious voice.

"You've never heard the story of Einstein staying out on the North Fork of Long Island in the summertime? Back in the 1930s, I think. He would try sailing but would get all tangled up. Local people had to jump in the water and rescue him sometimes."

Jesse clearly loved to share his knowledge. His enthusiasm and descriptions almost made it seem as though he was talking about people he met and sees regularly. He had a real knack for bringing history to life.

"Did you know Einstein sent a letter from eastern Long Island to President Franklin Roosevelt in August 1939 about how an atomic bomb could be built and that the Germans were likely already at work on one? He pointed out the importance of uranium in making such a bomb and that the Germans had actually stopped the sale of uranium from Czechoslovakian mines that it had taken over."

"I had heard something about that," said Geo. "Amazing to think that such an historic letter was written out this way— and right near the beach of all places."

"Yes," said the librarian. "Such an unassuming man in such a relaxed setting. And there he was sitting by the bay thinking about atomic bombs and nuclear energy: bombs that could level cities and energy that now supplies us with so much of the electricity we use. Really amazing."

I had not thought of it all that way and did not know that Einstein sent that letter from eastern Long Island in the 1930s. It was sobering to think about.

"I think I will confine my studies to learning more about Chase and his paintings for now," said Geo.

"No problem," replied Jesse. "Let me show you the section where you can find books on Dutch influence and the books on Chase."

A short while later we were back in the car heading toward a diner Geo always goes to in Southampton on Hampton Road; it's a timeless place that has been there for decades. Like many diners or ice cream shops built years ago, its interior is all full of shiny surfaces, efficient order, and special appliances for preparing food that in most cases you don't eat every day. At one time, spaces like this must have seemed very modern. It's ironic we now find a homey comfort in them. Perhaps something about their layout and how what you have ordered is made just steps away in full view prompts a more human level of interaction with the staff.

Before long we were seated in a booth and ordered some food. I asked for mint ice cream. The place was famous for its ice cream.

Other customers included what looked like an overworked executive enjoying time away from his office by reading the business news by himself at the counter. His pale skin, black tasseled loafers, and pinkish red shorts gave him away as a busy city dweller with limited time off in the Hamptons, despite the brave attempts of the parade of whales that circled his cloth belt to convince observers that he was a permanent fixture of the nautical scene. There was also a pair of men who seemed to be on a break from some tough physical job outside, judging from their clothes, worn and dirty baseball caps, and their boots. Their deep tans suggested roofing might be a good guess as to their line of work. Clearly, eating big sandwiches on toasted bread and reviewing the latest baseball scores is how they would rather spend their time.

But figuring out their story was not our focus. Geo and I started going over our new clues for the mystery we were most interested in solving. "What do you make of it all?" asked Geo.

"Well," I answered. "We know some lady has an interest in what we are doing. We know there are two umbrellas on both the map and in a painting from the 1890s. We know that the local folks did not think much about Einstein's sailing skills in the 1930s. He played a violin, and there is a violin and a sailboat on the map."

"The clues point to the water and the beach."

"It would seem that somewhere around Peconic Bay, which is right in front of your house and where the map was found, is looking like a smart place to focus."

Geo, who was facing the window that looked out onto the street, stopped eating and seemed to be staring off. He was looking over my shoulder as if watching something outside.

"What is it?" I asked.

"I just saw it again."

"Saw what?"

"The color orange out of the corner of my eye. I think someone in an orange shirt just passed in front of this diner for the second time."

"The lady in the orange shirt?"

"I don't know," Geo answered. "But she could have followed us here and then saw our car parked in the street. Let's not hang around here too long."

Thirty minutes later, we were back at Geo's house with the map and our new clues. We spent the next few hours comparing the map Geo found on the beach with a nautical map of the area. We also gazed at the image of the Chase painting in the book we checked out from the library and conducted searches on Einstein and the summers he spent on the North Fork of Long Island. We took turns until lunch looking at the maps, the books, and the computer. We felt like we were getting close to something, but the path was still not clear.

William Merritt Chase lived in Shinnecock Hills in the late 1800s. Not far from Geo's house. If the two umbrellas on the map had anything to do with the William Merritt Chase painting, then the map might have something to do with this very beach. Did the violin and sailboat have anything to do with Einstein? We found on the map the place where Einstein spent the summers, Nassau Point on the north fork of Long

Island. That means across Peconic Bay. But there was something important to remember: we were sitting right on **Great** Peconic Bay. Einstein spent summers on **Little** Peconic Bay, east of here. That's on the other side of Robins Island, which we could see clearly from Geo's house. There was the Dutch word "groot," meaning "great" on the map. That was a good sign, but again we were facing the same issue: we could not see how the shapes on the map matched the contours of the water or land around here.

" I wonder," said Geo, "if whoever made this map—if that is what it is—did not want it to look too obviously like a real map. Perhaps we are supposed to focus on the words and drawings and symbols. If that is the case, then we could consider the violin and sailboat as representing the north shore of Little Peconic Bay. That would put the two umbrellas over where we are. Right by this beach. That much would match."

This idea of Geo's got me thinking. It hit me while looking at the Chase painting. Why hadn't I thought of it before?! At least this new idea could provide more clues, if my hunch turned out right.

Chapter Four

The Return of the Dog On the Beach

"I am going to take a walk down the beach," I announced. "I think the scene in the Chase painting looks familiar. Something about it."

"Okay," said Geo. "But don't start ruining the beach by digging holes everywhere looking for Captain Kidd's buried treasure!" he teased me. "It is easy to get caught up in dreams and lose your focus on solving the real puzzle here. This 'map' thing is not old enough to be Kidd's treasure map anyway. You know that. Also, be careful—I still don't know what to make of that mysterious lady in the library." He looked concerned. I wondered what he figured this lady might be up to and why she might be following us. I just thought she was weird and that we would not see her again.

I headed down the beach, walking east. It didn't take me long to get to where I thought the painting would look familiar. Sure enough, I found just the right spot on the beach. It looked like the setting for the Chase painting. And just as I had expected, the land in the background of the Chase painting must be Robins Island! I had used my imagination and discovered something concrete.

I sometimes have a hard time processing scenes in old paintings, in this case a painting from the 1800s.[2] Something about a whole different way of life and interacting with others that can be hard to imagine. There they sit wearing an incredible amount of clothes on a sunny day at the beach. They, likely the family of Chase, the artist, are wearing hats and long dresses, while sitting under giant umbrellas. And these are not just any old hats. They are busy hats that seem to have decorations, perhaps flowers, on them. But maybe they were very wise. After all, we seemed to have relearned these days the importance of protection from the sun. These folks surely took that seriously.

More importantly, I was fascinated with how over one hundred years ago they sat on the same beach I have always hung out on. They enjoyed the same scenery and the same atmosphere by the shore. And today they handed me a key clue.

This was exciting, but we still had far to go in solving this mystery. As we knew from the start, there was no clear X on the

---

2   Just a reminder that you will find an image of this painting, *At the Seaside*, on the back cover of this book.

map. So, even if we were right that the two umbrellas indicated the south shore of Great Peconic Bay, where Geo lived, and the violin and sailboat indicated the north shore of Little Peconic Bay, we still did not know what we were looking for or where it was. I was frustrated.

To help myself think, I headed further down the beach, away from Geo's house. There was an *M* on the map in this direction. I had no clue what that might mean, and it was hard to tell how far down the beach, if it was even on the beach, this was supposed to be. I figured walking would help me think, and besides, what else could we do? It could not hurt to explore a little, I thought. Clouds persisted, and it felt cooler. The wind picked up as well as I walked. I hoped Geo was wrong and that the lady in the library was not really following us.

About twenty minutes later I came to a small inlet. Water from Great Peconic Bay moved back and forth through a channel with the tides, in and out of a huge network of ponds. The tide seemed to be coming in slowly. I had not yet passed anything that seemed like it should be represented by the letter *M* if one was making a map, but I had come this far. I wanted to keep going. It got darker as more serious-looking clouds moved in.

I swam across a small inlet and kept walking. I walked for what seemed like a long time. As time went on, I began feeling tired and frustrated. It was nothing but a hunch, some strange faith, that got Geo and me onto the trail of this mystery.

Reaching a dead end like this made me start to doubt this "map" was really anything at all. I wondered how much we were wasting our time.

I looked around the beach on this side, the east side, of the inlet. I had never been here before. There were no houses, but there was plenty of beach grass and old, weathered signs around the perimeter warning people to stay out. It was a bird sanctuary, but everyone was allowed to walk down the beach. Feeling like a gambler who has lost over and over again but still thinks he can win, I decided to keep heading down the lonely beach, which curved for miles eastward.

I walked along with the Great Peconic Bay on my left and the grassy bird-zone on my right. It was a narrow strip of land, and on the other side of the bird-zone was a huge pond. I did not remember its name but had seen it on maps many times before. I looked up and saw that the terrain was different up ahead. Hills covered in low trees and brush would start soon— replacing what had been the grassy bird-zone. I squinted my eyes in the hope that somehow the shapes of the land or of the trees would somehow look like an *M*, but they didn't. There was no one around as far as I could see, or so I thought.

My first hint that I was not alone was the sound of footsteps coming from the other side of the grassy area on my right. I would stop now and then and listen, but the footsteps would also stop. Perhaps I was just hearing things. Whatever it was, it was moving in the grass near me.

I was standing still on the beach now and could hear the wind and my heart beating. I was petrified. I was absolutely afraid to move. Somehow I felt that if I moved, whatever it was would...I didn't know what to think.

I found myself running away down the beach. I ran and ran, looking ahead to keep my footing and thinking that each step was critical. I could hear, almost feel, something right at my heels. I was afraid to turn and lose my footing, but I tripped anyway in the sand and rocks. Before I knew it I was rolling forward on the ground. I saw the sky and the ground and the sky and the ground and sky again as I tumbled. I remember feeling the sand in my mouth and fearing what would happen next.

I was face down in the sand and no longer moving, but my head spun from the dizziness as if I was still tumbling. I tried to look behind me to see what was chasing me and how close it was and felt sick from the dizziness. A big, black shape—like a bear—was walking toward me in a determined way. I tried to get to my feet but found that the world was spinning in my head. I fell as I tried to get up. The creature approached. I shut my eyes in a desperate attempt to stop the spinning sensation. I held up my arm to protect my body from being bitten.

The next thing I knew I was being licked by a huge dog's tongue. The creature—a giant-sized canine, perhaps a Newfoundland—started with my outstretched arm and then moved right to my face, licking the whole time. His huge tail wagged back and forth, generating a rush of air around us.

I was in a state of terror one second and then treated like a long-lost brother the next! The huge dog got happier the more I relaxed, wagging his tail and licking my face the whole time.

He was a giant and wore no collar, just a blue bandana tied around his neck. And he drooled quite a bit. I could see no other person in any direction. "Take it easy, big fella," I said to him, gently pushing him away from me. He sat and looked at me, panting and full of expectation. "Where did you come from? Can you show me?" He turned his head as I asked my questions but just sat there, looking as if he was hoping we were about to do something fun. It would take me some effort to find his tracks because he came by way of the grass. I looked up and down the beach and thought I saw an area where the embankment was lower and there was less grass. Perhaps this was a place I could cut through and get to the pond side of the strip of land.

"Come on, pal," I gestured for him to follow as I headed toward this break in the embankment. He walked along next to me with his head up, looking at my face and with his tail wagging, as if he was waiting for me to say a certain command that he knew. "Come," I said. "Good boy." I encouraged him to follow at my side as we made our way through the break in the dune. Thirty feet ahead of us we could see the huge pond whose name I had forgotten. It was ringed by tall reeds, and there were ducks and geese cruising on the surface. There were even a few swans, whose bright white feathers stood out in what was still a less-than-colorful scene because of the clouds.

My new friend jogged ahead of me. I hoped he might reveal where he had come from or perhaps who had brought him here by retracing his own steps, but this was not the route he took to follow me. There were no dog or people tracks to see yet, just lots of what looked like bird tracks.

I looked up and down the shore of the pond. I doubted he came from the west, the direction of the inlet, but I could not be sure. The beach stretched a long way down and curved. There could be someone way down by the inlet or in the grass. Looking the other way, to the east, I saw what looked like large, smooth, round rocks glistening in the sun a short way down the shore. Some looked as though they were the diameter of a basketball. *How strange*, I thought. I started walking toward them and my canine pal came lumbering up behind me and, once again, started to lead the way.

He stopped before the huge zone of rocks and froze in his tracks. His tail stopped wagging, and he held it straight up. As I came up behind him, I could hear a low growl coming from deep in his chest. He kept very still. His growl got louder. And then louder. He tossed in a bark every few seconds. What was it that made him nervous? I looked ahead to the field of rocks—and one of them moved.

"You silly boy! It's all right," I laughed and stroked his back. "Those are just horseshoe crabs! There sure are a lot of them, huh?" I petted him some more. He had stopped barking, and his tail wagged a bit at the sound of my voice, but he was still on alert. I had never seen so many horseshoe crabs in my life in one place.

Horseshoe crabs are unusual. They look very dangerous and intimidating: a dome-like round shell of a body with a tail like a dagger sticking out behind them. Their round shells move through the sand on legs hidden underneath.

They look as though they are from outer space, but the truth is that they are shy and relatively harmless. They crawl on the floor of the bay and along the shore with their dagger-like tail just dragging along behind them. You would have to go out of your way to step on the tail and get seriously hurt. They don't sting or carry poison. Still, this was quite a sight with so many of them.

More interesting to me was what I saw in the water. A sandbar went right from the shore out into the expansive pond toward what looked like a small rocky, treeless island. It reminded me of why I was here. The small island would be just the place to bury treasure, if that was what this was all about. Perhaps the rocks might turn out to be in the shape of an *M*— one of the clues from the map. Besides, I might be able to see the whole shore better from there and perhaps could find the owner of this big, friendly dog. It might even be a person who will know something about the box and map we found. In the back of my mind, I had not given up on the notion that there would be some treasure at the end of my search. This vision gave me the motivation to press on.

I started wading through the shallow water. It looked as though the island was about one hundred yards off shore. Slowly, the pond got deeper. I could feel a current against my legs as I marched forward. The big, black dog tried to stay at my side but waited for me to move first. He was not leading the way this time. We pushed onward through the water. As the water level started to get a bit higher, my canine pal resorted to half jumping, half swimming. We were almost there now.

With a big spray of water, the dog shook himself to dry off once we were on the beach—his wet bandana still hanging around his neck. He started sniffing everything. I looked around for anything interesting—a pattern in some of the larger rocks, some markings, or some other sign. Nothing looked like it was in an *M* shape. Nor were there any *X* shapes. I spent about half an hour walking along what was really just a little circle of rocky beach out in the water. My new furry friend was fascinated with all the smells. Then I noticed something strange.

I was looking so carefully at the terrain that I was bound to notice this. In half an hour, the island had gotten much smaller. Much, much smaller. "Of course," I thought, "high tide is coming in!" I have never seen the water rise so quickly. And come to think of it, this might explain why there are no trees and such little beach grass. This island gets covered with lots of water at high tide. Just then, I noticed that the current had gotten much stronger between the island and the shore where the horseshoe crabs had gathered.

My canine companion stopped a minute or two earlier and listened, watching the shore of the beach near where the horse-shoe crabs were. As if he heard or saw some signal, he jumped into the water and swam for the shore we had come from. His speed and strength were impressive. I could not see his back legs in action as they were underwater, but one thing was clear—he was a very strong swimmer. His speed was remark-able, and he followed generally a straight line with the current pushing his path at a slight angle. I watched in amazement as he reached the other shore and, again, generated a cloud of spray with a great shake of his furry coat. He headed off into the beach grass as if he saw something or someone. As amazing as this was, I was still on the island, which was getting smaller by the minute as the tide quickly rose and the current seemed to get stronger.

I started to make an emergency plan. I could always just float in the current if the water started to go above the level of the island. The current was bound to take me toward one of the nearby beaches; the pond was almost surrounded by land. The trick was not to panic.

The island was getting smaller and smaller as the tide rose. It became clear to me now that it was entirely covered in water when the tide was high. It was just a matter of time before it would be submerged. I scanned the horizon to see if there were any boats nearby.

Across the pond I could just make out a low boat and the dull, regular sound of its engine. I think I might have unconsciously heard the engine before I saw it and, as I listened, could now hear it getting louder. It was headed near where I was standing. I don't think the person on the boat saw me yet, but he or she was headed this way and perhaps going toward the inlet and out into the bay.

After about ten minutes, the fishing boat came much closer. I could see a man with a wide-brimmed, dark blue hat and sunglasses sitting in the back of the boat as he operated the outboard engine, which looked like a black box attached to the rear of the boat from the distance I was at. I waved my arms and shouted. It wasn't long before he saw me and was very clearly headed my way.

He came close to the island—the part that was still sticking out above the surface of the pond—and recognized I was in a tough spot. I swam a bit toward his boat and pulled myself over the side. The boat smelled like fish and was filled with gear—fishing gear and crab traps. "What were you doing out there anyway?" the man asked in a quiet, almost muffled voice, once I was aboard his boat and seated. I sat in the bow some distance from where he was in the stern. A huge pile of gear separated us.

"I was exploring and walked out to that little island along a sandbar. Before I knew it, conditions had changed," I explained.

"You really have to watch the tides and currents. That's how people drown," he admonished me.

We introduced ourselves. His name was Willie. I explained where Geo lived and where I needed to get back to. Willie agreed to give me a ride to Geo's pier since he was headed toward the Shinnecock Canal and Geo's was on the way.

In an effort to find out more about area I had been exploring, I described for Willie where I had walked to see if it would prompt any interesting information from him. I told him about the mysterious dog, but he did not seem familiar with it at all. As I described where I had been walking, he interrupted me.

"So, you were in the land of the living fossils, eh?" he asked with a smile.

"Living fossils? What do you mean?" I answered, some-what confused by what he was asking.

"Those crabs. You must have seen lots of them. You know, the horseshoe crabs."

"Yes, I saw the largest number I had ever seen on the beach before I headed out to explore that little island," I explained. "Why do you call them 'living fossils'?"

He seemed a little surprised that I was not familiar with this nickname. "They were around during the age of the dino-saurs," he explained. "Actually, scientists say they have not changed much in the past four hundred million years. That's two hundred million years before the dinosaurs."

I was stunned. I had seen these creatures for decades along the beaches in the Hamptons but did not know about their history. It was remarkable to think they had survived this way for so long.

They were miraculous survivors, carrying on from one generation to the next for four hundred million years; they seemed so tough and fragile at the same time. Then it hit me; these are the "dinosaurs" from the map!

Wow! I nearly jumped out of the boat when I thought of it. *Won't Geo be interested in this information?!*

Chapter Five

Exploring New Clues

Half an hour later I was back at Geo's, all thanks to Willie. He dropped me off at Geo's dock and was on his way. Not only did he save me from getting caught in a rapidly rising tide and provide me with a ride home, but he also gave us a new clue. Geo was not home, and his car was gone, likely off tracking down new leads.

"Horseshoe crabs! Of course!" Geo exclaimed hours later when I told him. "That's what the word 'dinosaurs' on the map might mean! I have heard that people refer to them as living fossils."

It seemed we had a new clue, but I was to learn that Geo had made some headway himself in his travels around the area by car and in the hours I was gone.

"If the umbrellas have to do with this beach because of what we figured with the William Merritt Chase painting, and if the violin and sailboat indicate the north shore of Little Peconic Bay where Einstein used to spend the summer, not only does it make sense that the area you were in with the horseshoe crabs matches the spot where it says 'dinosaurs' on the map, BUT I have noticed something else," he said proudly. "If we are interpreting this map correctly so far, then the map is written upside down compared to a standard map. In the case of the one I found, the top is south and the bottom is north."

This did not surprise me all that much, but I was not sure what it told us. Sensing my question, Geo continued. "That would mean the *M* on this map is meant to be read the other way. It might be a *W*." It looked as though Geo was on to something here. Indeed, the *M*, if you turned the map, could be read as a *W*.

Not that anything obvious came to mind now for either one of us, but at the very least it opened the door to new opportunities. We could now keep our eyes peeled for significant *W*s and our minds thinking about what the letter *W* might stand for. I had just gone on a small adventure thinking the whole time about the letter *M*. Hopefully, my mind would have noticed the similar *W* shape if it had been there in the rocks on the island or somewhere else in the terrain where I had walked today.

"I have more good news," Geo announced. "A friend of mine is going to visit any minute. She is very good at crossword puzzles. I think she will help us with other aspects of the map."

Just then someone rang the hanging bell that was attached to the wall next to Geo's door. Geo went to see who it was and returned to his living room with an older lady. She looked about seventy years old. Perhaps eighty.

"This is Nancy," Geo introduced her. "She is an expert at all sorts of word puzzles. You can always find Nancy with a crossword puzzle in hand." Nancy waved away his compliments and sat down.

"Geo said you boys found some old piece of paper with strange words on it," Nancy said. "I would be happy to look at it and do what I can. Anything is better than heading into town at this hour. All the summer people drive like crazy when they come out here. Makes going to the supermarket a real head-ache. I really cannot wait for the summer to be over," she said with all seriousness.

It was not clear how much Geo had told Nancy. She frankly did not seem very interested in where the "piece of paper" was found or anything else about it. As Geo had stated, and she was soon to demonstrate, she liked word puzzles. She just focused on the words. I guess when you are used to crossword puzzles that are created by someone who just selects the questions and integrates the answers on a grid, you don't spend much time thinking about "why answer this question?" or "where did the puzzle come from?" Instead, you simply enjoy the challenge of coming up with the answer no matter how obscure the questions may be.

Geo handed her a clean sheet of paper that had just two words from the map: "groot" and "xjtdpotjo." Nancy looked them over for about three seconds.

"Well that 'groot' looks like Dutch. Dutch for 'great.'"

"'Great' like 'Great Peconic Bay,' for example?" asked Geo.

"Yes," answered Nancy, looking out Geo's huge window at the bay before us. "A Dutch word like *robbe* or *robben*."

"What's that?" both Geo and I asked about the same time.

"Oh come on! What's the matter with you two? *Robben!*" she exclaimed as if simply repeating it would help us understand. "Right in front of you! You haven't heard that word?! And you live around here?"

Geo and I looked at each other half confused and half amused that she was so insistent it was obvious to everyone.

"Oh, you two need all the help you can get, don't you?" she asked indignantly. "Right there!" She pointed out the window, seemingly at the bay.

"Is that the Dutch word for 'bay'?" I asked cautiously.

"Ohhh, please! Now you are just kidding me!" she said, seeming to think we were playing dumb, but we weren't. "You both know Robins Island. Right over there. *Robbe* or *robben* comes from the Dutch word for 'seal.' There were probably lots of seals over there years ago, but you two knew that, of course!"

Geo and I were excited at this revelation and laughed hard. Nancy thought it was because she caught us playing dumb. "Stop pulling my leg!" she chided us.

"What else do you know about Robins Island?" Geo asked. "I bet there are many things we don't know about it."

"Well, I am no expert. But I heard that it was owned by some man who sided with England in the Revolutionary War. Some guy named Wickham. The American colonies took it away from him and banished him from the estate. It was then put up for sale and purchased by two of George Washington's associates. I forget who owns it now."

"Interesting," said Geo. "So 'groot' sounds Dutch, huh? What do you make of the other word?"

Nancy thought hard. "It doesn't look like any word I have seen in my crosswords. I cannot figure out what language it might be. Hmmm. It almost looks like a code."

"A code?" I asked.

"Yes, it is either some obscure language, or it is a code of some sort." Nancy started doodling on the page. She kept going for about ten minutes as Geo and I paced around the living room, letting her work. "Well, there we have it," she finally said. "Not as sophisticated as those General Washington's army used."

"What did you figure out?" Geo asked excitedly.

"It looks to me like a simple substitution cipher. That's a puzzle where someone replaces one letter of the alphabet for another. Puzzles like this have been used since the time of Caesar and are sometimes called 'Caesar's ciphers.' General Washington used them also. But this was the simplest you can have. Just replace each letter here with the letter before it in the alphabet."

We looked at what Nancy had written. Lots of notes and the alphabet and "xjtdpotjo"—the word from the map.

"And what does it all add up to?" I asked.

Nancy showed me what she came up with after solving the puzzle. Substituting each letter in the weird word on the map with the letter before it in the alphabet, she came up with a recognizable word. I was stunned when I looked at the answer. Did this answer to the puzzle mean we were not even in the right part of the country?

~~~

End of Part One

Part Two

⌘

Red Sky at Night,
Sailors' Delight.
Red Sky in Morning,
Sailors Take Warning.

–Ancient mariners' adage

Chapter Six

A Setback?

"Wisconsin!" Geo and I shouted together. Nancy had found that by substituting each letter of the strange word on the map for the letter before it in the alphabet we had "Wisconsin."

How could that be? We thought we were hot on the trail and coming up with clues that seemed to indicate that map was pointing to something on eastern Long Island, and now this! Wisconsin is a whole other state hundreds of miles from New York. How could the map be of Wisconsin! We were in shock. At the same time, it was too complicated to explain the whole thing to Nancy. After all, we had simply asked her to solve a puzzle. And she did this supremely well. Geo got himself together quickly, recovering from the shock.

"Excellent, Nancy!" Geo said with a big smile. "We would have never been able to figure this out on our own."

"Yes," I regained my composure, "you really are remarkable in the way you did that so quickly."

Nancy felt very proud of herself, as she should have. Geo started some tea and brought out a big crumb cake for us all to enjoy. We spent the next hour or so eating crumb cake and listening to Nancy share her tricks for solving word puzzles. She then got up to leave. "My grandchildren will be visiting this afternoon. I should get back home so that I don't miss them." As soon as she left, we slumped onto the couch in the living room so that we could survey where we were in our journey in solving this mystery.

"Wisconsin!" I later exclaimed for at least the tenth time. "What is going on? This is very frustrating." We weren't sure what we had here. "We thought we were uncovering clues that could make some sort of sense and point to this area. Now this! Wisconsin is far from here!"

"It doesn't look good," said Geo. "But let's not give up. I cannot believe those clues aren't pointing to this area, and now we have Robins Island matching the seal on the map as well. That's too much of a coincidence for this to turn out to be some map pointing to a whole other part of the country."

"Right!" I said, feeling somewhat reinvigorated after what seemed like a bad turn in the path.

But it was getting later. We poked around on the Internet and kept exploring opportunities until we got so tired we called it a night.

I was up early the next morning to a sky lit red by a murky shape that was the dawning sun. I found Geo was already up and back at the computer. "Over here," said Geo, walking toward his computer. "Let's see if the word 'Wisconsin' might mean something for this area. It's a long shot, but we have nothing to lose, do we?" He put "Wisconsin" and "Long Island" into a search engine. We were surprised to see there is a place called Long Island in the state of Wisconsin. This could mean all the clues we have been seeing were partly our imagination and that this map refers to some other place entirely. We spent a good part of the day brainstorming.

I finally had an idea: my work in meteorology has made me very aware of global warming issues. I suddenly had a trace memory of why the word "Wisconsin" might be relevant. I added some key words to the search. That did the trick.

We both read a key page at the same time. It said,

> About 18,000 years ago, Connecticut, the Long Island Sound, and much of Long Island were covered by a thick sheet of ice, part of what is called the Late Wisconsin Glacier. About 1,000 meters thick in its interior and about 400 to 500 meters thick along its southern edge, it was the most recent of a series of glaciations that covered the area during the past 10 million years.

"Of course!" shouted Geo. "That's it! The glacier story! The whole North Fork of Long Island is a huge deposit of soil and rocks that were carried by a glacier thousands of years ago! One of those glaciers was later called the 'Wisconsin' glacier! The word 'Wisconsin' on the map is right next to the dotted line on the map. That line shows how far the glacier advanced and refers to the north shore of this bay! We're back on the trail!"

This was a huge relief to hear that there was a chance we were still closing in on something. We ran back over to the living room table to look at the map. Our clues were all taking shape. Except one thing—we didn't have an X on the map. It was starting to look like we could decode all the clues, but there was no clear arrow pointing in one direction or one spot on the map that looked more important than any other. This had us stumped.

"I think," said Geo, after about twenty minutes of us pondering and debating, "that the W—or is it an M after all?—on this map is the focal point. We know what locations the other clues symbolize. We need to head east of here and figure out what might be connected with an M or W."

We lost no time in gathering our gear—maps, cell phones, notes we had made—and headed for Geo's car. As we drove, we thought hard about features of the area that start with an M or a W. Up and down the roads we went, looking for a good candidate to help us solve the mystery. At first we were filled with excitement, but before long we started to run out of steam. What to do next?

"Let's stop for a late lunch in town," said Geo. "We need to think again. Perhaps we'll even swing by the library again and talk with Jesse. He knows so much and may have an idea."

I knew where Geo had in mind for lunch. He always likes to go to one of a handful of places. Somehow following routines helps him think. "Are we headed to the Southampton Publick House?" I asked with a smile.

"How did you guess?" he replied.

Before long we arrived at the Southampton Publick House and were walking under its long awning into the bustling dining room and were seated at a table. This restaurant has a central location in Southampton, and the building it occupies has had a long history of welcoming people. Decades ago movie stars and prominent personalities all stopped here for dinner and dancing. Today, it is less formal but no less active. The addition of a brewery has added to both the menu and its festive atmosphere, but we would have to pass on having beer this time since we had serious thinking to do. We ate and talked and talked and ate. Running up and down a list of words that begin with *M*, like *mill*, *meadow*, *museum*, and then mulling over words that start with *W*, like *whale*, *water*, *wampum*. As much as we enjoyed taking the break, we got more frustrated as we went on. We could not think of one candidate for a known feature in the area that started with *M* or *W* and that fit the map. It had to be someplace near the water, especially one of the bays.

"What do you say we swing back to the library?" Geo asked rhetorically, and left money on the table to pay the bill.

We headed for the door. As we left I looked carefully at some of the paintings and photos on the walls for inspiration. Something made me stop.

"I might be on to something," I announced to Geo. "Look at this."

There was an illustration on the wall of a windmill and near it several old black-and-white photos of windmills.

"Windmills?" Geo asked and then caught himself. "Oh! Windmills! Right. Starts with a *W*! We did not think of windmills. There are a number of them out here on the East End of Long Island. Of course!"

"Yup. But the trick will be to find one by the water. There is one over by the college, but that is too far from the shore. Let's swing by and talk with Jesse at the library."

We were at the Rogers Memorial Library in minutes as it is just down the street. Jesse was amused to see us back there with our unusual questions, but he also seemed happy that he had a chance to share his knowledge of the area again. "I think there are about eleven old windmills still standing on the East End of Long Island," he said pensively. "But one near the water? Hmmm… And keep in mind a number of them have been moved from their original sites, if that makes any difference to you.

The one in Bridgehampton, for example, was almost moved to Brooklyn about a hundred years ago, but then they realized they would not be able to transport it, so it stayed out on the East End. It was originally built near the water and has been moved a few times."

"It was near the water long ago?" I asked, thinking out loud.

"Yes. As a matter of fact, when it was near the bay, there was an old saying: 'A flag on the mill, a ship in the bay.' This was because the windmill acted as a sort of signal tower. A flag would be placed on the top of the windmill to signal that a ship was entering the bay and returning from the sea. The windmill was a real focal point for the community."

"Just because they would hang flags from it when a ship was arriving?"

"It was more than that," Jesse responded. "People would gather there, and news would be shared. You see, these windmills played a crucial role in the daily lives of most people. Folks would grow their crops and then bring the grain to the windmill, and the grain would be ground down to flour by the huge mill stones. The mill stones, of course, would turn by wind power."

"I keep forgetting what their original role was," I confessed. "To me they are romantic structures that make me feel nostalgic, but really they were an important machine and helped people make a basic food item, bread. Also, many depictions of the windmills don't show them with the sails set up.

These windmills had huge sails that turned the blades when the wind blew, didn't they?"

"Yes, that's right. Some of the windmills had a revolving top floor so that the blades, with their sails, could be pointed into the wind. That way they could keep milling grain no matter which way the wind came from. Sometimes people would build a mill that would use water power. Water would turn a paddle that would rotate a wheel connected to the mill stone. That's where Watermill, the area not far from here, gets its name."

"If we are looking for one that is still near the water today, what would be our best bet?" Geo asked.

"I've got it. Of course! There is Windmolen," Jesse said excitedly. "Over by Peconic Bay. But, I have to say, no one really knows the history of that windmill. It is sort of a mystery how it got there or how long it has been there."

Both Geo and I knew about Windmolen but had forgotten about it in the excitement. It stood on hill in an undeveloped area near the bay. We thanked Jesse and headed to the car.

It took us about twenty minutes to drive along back roads to the area of Windmolen as the late day sky prematurely darkened with storm clouds. It was tough as we tried to remember the way to the old windmill. We were in a neighborhood of lots of dead ends because the area was basically the shoreline of the huge pond I saw earlier in the day. So some roads just went right down to the water and ended as a type of boat ramp. There were many, many houses and stretches of tall beach grass.

We were about to pass one street when Geo pulled over to the side of the road. "Isn't the old munitions dump down this street? The dump not too far from the shore of the Great Peconic Bay?"

"Munitions dump? I have never heard of such a thing," I answered.

"Apparently, there is an old field not too far from the shore where they used to dump old World War II bombs and explosives. It became a big deal years ago when environmental groups started warning about the danger of the explosives and the chemicals."

"Really?" I wondered out loud. "My family has been out this way for many decades. How is this the first I have ever heard of this? All I remember is that old windmill on the hill." Geo turned down Windmolen Drive, down toward the water.

I could feel the car accelerate as Geo drove forward. He got very quiet and focused on driving down the twisting street and looking around. We both looked around with new purpose as we sped down the curvy, tree-lined street.

Suddenly, the trees on the side of the road became fewer, and there was a beach on one side of us and a view of Great Peconic Bay. Sitting dramatically at the top of the hill was the old windmill in silhouette against the darkening sky as storm clouds continued to move in, but the road up the hill was still a distance ahead. Meanwhile, we passed a variety of unpaved roads that headed off into the trees. Geo stopped at one of them.

"Here," he said, "is the entrance to the old munitions dump."

"Here?" I asked in disbelief. I remembered playing around this area as a kid but had no memory of a dangerous weapons dump. There were signs now with skulls and crossbones that warned people away because of the danger.

"I think something fishy is going on here," said Geo. "It has been on my mind for a while. I have a bad feeling now that our search has led us to this area...a very bad feeling." He started the car again and headed right up the road toward the dump and past the warning signs.

"Where are we going?" I asked in disbelief.

"We need to see what is up ahead." It was getting darker now as the sun began to sink into the bay.

But our path ended at a barbed-wire fence that was locked up tight. There was a boarded-up building. The road continued into the trees. Geo turned the car around to go back to Windmolen Drive, but on our way back, he noticed a side road that we had not noticed entering because of the way it is hidden by the trees. He pulled into it. The bushes and trees were overgrown, almost touching the car as we drove along slowly. It led right back to the main road of the munitions dump in one big loop in the woods. Geo turned back onto the driveway to get back down to Windmolen Drive.

As Geo turned back onto the main driveway-like road, a pair of headlights suddenly appeared behind us, but they were not from a car. It was a large truck moving fast. "Hang on," Geo said. He pressed on the accelerator, but somehow the truck seemed to be right on our rear bumper the whole time. Geo went faster, but the truck went faster still. We would be coming up to Windmolen Drive soon but going too fast to turn right or left safely. The truck looked as though it was trying to hit us from behind to send us spinning. "Hold on tight," Geo said. "I have an idea."

We would be coming up to the intersection any second. I was praying there would be no cars on Windmolen Drive because we would crash right into them. Even if there weren't any cars, how were we going to stop? Suddenly, the intersection was right in front of us. I held my breath.

All I remember seeing is the neatly paved road of Windmolen Drive right in front of us going right and left. There was enough visibility to see there were no cars coming—lucky break. But still, we were speeding. Way too fast!

It was just then that I saw directly in front of us was a narrow dirt road that led down to the water. Geo shot across Windmolen Drive, and we were bouncing down the dirt road headed right for the boat ramp. The huge truck did not cross Windmolen Drive as smoothly but still was bearing down at high speed behind us, getting closer each second. Now we faced a new problem: we were headed right for the boat ramp, right into the bay. Geo was focused but did not panic. He almost seemed somehow satisfied with himself. Both our car and the mysterious truck were speeding fast down the dirt road. I will never forget what happened next.

Geo barely slowed at all. I think he just took his foot off the gas and aimed straight into the water. Just before we hit the water, he started flipping switches fast. "Don't get out of the car!" he shouted. "Stay right where you are unless I tell you otherwise." The car slowed suddenly as it hit the water but then jerked forward. I was ready to feel the jolt of the truck hitting us from behind. I then realized something in the twilight: the car was moving fast across the surface of the water, like a boat! Geo had built some sort of boat-car!

"I modified this car a bit," Geo said smugly. "I was inspired by an Amphicar and some of those other amphibious vehicles."

I looked back to see the exhaust puffing out of vents just behind the rear window of Geo's car. Deck lights lit up the hood and truck lid in red and green. There we were cruising through the water like any motor boat.

Geo never ceases to surprise and amaze me. He quietly works on his many projects slowly over time and often comes up with the most impressive devices. This one, though, has to top them all. A car you can drive right into the water! I thought the car had, in some respects, the lines of a boat. I never thought to actually ask him if somehow a boat had inspired the work he was doing on it. And I never once thought to look under the chassis to see if there was any means to propel it through the water.

"This car has propellers underneath?" I shouted over the now louder engine.

"Yup. Just like an Amphicar, but I'll tell you more later. We have enough to do at the moment."

Then, from behind us, there was the tremendous WHAM of the truck hitting the water. I looked back saw it with its front end in the water and its back end rising into the air because of the momentum. I thought for a second that it was going to do a somersault, but the back end bounced down loudly and steam rose from the huge machine. It had gotten too dark for me to make out any people.

"Who were they, and why did they want to kill us? I don't know how anyone would survive in that truck," I rambled excitedly, countless thoughts going through my head at once.

"I have a hunch about who they are and what they are hiding. As far as the truck driver, I am not sure there was one. That might have simply been a truck sent rolling downhill to scare us off. They could always say it was an accident and that the brake was not applied properly, and it rolled downhill. That way they could try to claim innocence without really getting exposed to danger themselves. I am not sure that is even a munitions dump."

This was a lot for me to process after a terrifying ride. "What's next?"

"I think we need to keep going," Geo said. "Are you holding up okay?"

"I think so," I answered nervously.

Geo had been heading down the shore, closer to the base of the hill on which the windmill stood. Another boat ramp led back to Windmolen Drive. He aimed for it, accelerated across the water, and then, just as we got close to the ramp, I felt a jolt as the wheels found traction on the boat ramp. The car pulled itself out of the water, dripping everywhere.

It felt great to be back on solid ground. But we had new challenges ahead and not much time to think. Geo pointed to a path and said, "Take that route up toward the windmill. Just look around. Go quickly. I am not sure what you'll see, but the map seemed to be pointing here.

"I need you to head to the windmill as soon as possible and take a look around. I am going to call the police and get them over here. It might have been unreasonable to tell them about what looked like a lot of gibberish on a map, but they will have to listen to how we were almost killed by a 'runaway' truck, and there won't be enough time for anyone to pull that truck out of the water."

Geo had been heading down along the shore, closer to the base of the hill on which the windmill stood. We had new challenges ahead and not much time to think. Geo pointed to a path and said, "Take that route up toward the windmill. Just look around. Go quickly. I am not sure what you'll see, but the map seems to be pointing here. I am going to call the police. Take your cell phone, and call me the second you see anything strange."

I headed up the hill on the switchback trail that led up toward the windmill with my flashlight lighting my way.

The old windmill stood silently on the hill watching my progress. There were no lights on it or coming from it. It was eerie. It was just a dark shape. As I climbed the path, its silhouette stood out in the night sky as my eyes adjusted but then would become hidden by the trees after I made a turn. With each bend in the path, the old structure loomed larger. Finally, I made one more turn in the switchback path, and there was the old windmill waiting like a sleeping giant. There was Windmolen.

Windmolen stood in a level grassy area. I never saw it before as anything but a charming feature, simply part of the landscape. This adventure gave it a forbidding sense of mystery. Now it seemed like a volcano that hadn't erupted in many years but could at any moment. To add to the effect, the wind had picked up, and the weather was taking a turn for the worse. I even thought I felt a drop or two of rain.

I circled the outside of the base of the windmill. Besides one door and some writing on its foundation, there was not much to see. The huge blades for the sails reached out like giant arms but were motionless.

I walked up to the door and turned the latch. It opened with a terrible creak. I pointed my little flashlight inside and saw a narrow and dusty space and various wooden gears and levers. Also, there was a staircase.

I stepped inside. The door creaked shut behind me. I trained my light on the stairs. They were steep and narrow, more like a ladder with a handrail than like any staircase I was used to. I took a deep breath and could feel my heart beating. "Anyone in here?!" I shouted up the stairs.

There was no answer.

I stepped forward and began the steep climb, sometimes putting the flashlight in my mouth to hold onto the rails. The stairs creaked with each step. Up and up I went. I had no sense of how high I was at any moment. The windmill had several levels. I went from one to the next, navigating the shadows and large wooden gears that made up the machinery of the windmill, and that's when I heard a strange noise. It was like a scratching sound.

Scratch. Scratch. S-s-s-scraaatch.

I held my breath.

Again: Scratch. Scratch. S-s-s-scraaatch.

I pointed my flashlight straight up since the noise seemed to be coming from there. In the faint light I saw them. Scores of them. BATS. They clung to the ceiling in colonies and moved slowly around. I was not afraid of them because I felt I was on a mission.

I kept climbing the stairs. Finally, I reached the top. It was a small room covered in lots of dust. A huge wooden pole, almost like a mast of a ship, angled across the room. If Geo was worried there was someone trapped in here, they were not to be seen. Or so I thought—just then I saw what looked like a shadow move in the corner and noticed footprints in the dust. Someone WAS there.

My heart raced as a dark shape came toward me, almost silently. "What do you want?!" I shouted. The figure stopped. It was wearing a dark hood.

"What do YOU want?" the figure whispered.

I froze in place. I was not sure what to do. Head back down in the dark to the main level? Stay and find out who this was and what was going on?

Before I could move, the figure reached up and pulled back the hood. There in front of me was a woman in her thirties with long black hair—the lady from the library!

"Where is my grandfather?" she asked in a serious, angry tone. "Where is he?"

I was stunned. I wasn't expecting to see her. AND—I had no idea what she was talking about. "Your grandfather?"

"Why are you poking around here?"

"We found a type of map. We have been trying to figure out what it is about," I answered.

"Let me see the map," she demanded.

"I don't have it with me."

"Liar!" she shouted.

"I don't have it with me. I really don't," I answered.

She looked really sad and disappointed, as if she was about to cry. She was quiet for a moment or two and then started to tear up.

"I believe you," she managed to say through the tears. "I am just so tired and confused." She sat down on the floor of the room in the windmill, but just then we heard a noise down below. It was the sound of breathing and movement. I looked down the stairs, but all was darkness. The lady surprised me by smiling at this frightening moment.

"That's just Morgan looking for me," she said. "The big dog. You have met him already today by the pond. I saw you both head out to that island in the pond." We descended the old, narrow, creaky stairs carefully. Morgan was clearly happy to see us both—the lady and me, his new friend from earlier in the day. With a huge, wagging tail and giant, wet tongue he licked our faces and arms. Morgan circled us as if to offer a dance of joy at our return.

"I'm Paul," I said at last.

"I'm Lucy. I have been looking for my grandfather for several days. I think something has happened to him. He is seventy-five years old."

"Have you called the police?" I asked, reaching for my cell phone.

"That won't work around here," she said, nodding toward my phone. "There is no good cell phone coverage in this area. As far as my grandfather is concerned, I just have a feeling he is in trouble, and I am not sure who is behind it. I have been stepping very carefully trying to put together clues. You found something didn't you? That map. I have to see it. It might tell us where he is."

"What makes you think he is in trouble, rather than just staying with a friend? And why would he leave something like a map?"

"I don't live in this area. I got a call from my grandfather a few days ago. He left a voice-mail message asking me to visit. He then said that if anything happens to him, to look for the clues. I called and called, but he never answered the phone. I then came right away. His house was empty. Well, almost empty. Morgan was there, alone. My grandfather takes him everywhere, even in the boat." Lucy went on to explain that Morgan, a Newfoundland, is a powerful swimmer. His name is an old Celtic name that means "sea warrior," or "lives by the sea." The huge dog sat next to us, looking up at our faces expectantly.

"Who would want to hurt your grandfather?" I asked.

"I don't know, but I think it has to do with something he was looking for. Last year a friend of his from England came to visit. An old friend of his he met back in the 1940s. This man told my grandfather the answer to a riddle; I don't know exactly what, but since then my grandfather has been preoccupied. Roving around this area and going out in his boat, looking at the land from the water. He was very secretive about it. I am afraid he has met with some sort of trouble. I was led here by an idea I had. It seemed to make sense after the clue you let slip in the library—you asked about Dutch history. I have been hoping it has something to do with Windmolen, a Dutch name, and not the dangerous munitions dump next door. To top it all off, Morgan seems to be tracking something or someone in this area. That gave me hope."

I was amazed. Here she was, without the map, in the same place Geo and I had made our way to. I stood for a second taking it all in. She petted Morgan and scratched him on the neck, which he loved. I looked into the darkness in the direction of the field, toward the bordering fence. I knew that the property next door was surrounded by foreboding signs that said: "Warning—Keep Out. Dangerous Explosives and Mines." Each sign had a skull and crossbones, warning you away if you couldn't read. It sent a chill up my back. It was just then that we heard something.

Actually, it was Morgan's reaction that caused us to hear it. All of a sudden the huge dog stood up and looked toward the fence. It was then that I thought I heard someone yell, but it was a muffled sound. The wind had picked up, so it was hard to make out exactly. Again, I heard a muffled noise. Morgan was gone; he marched off into the darkening evening and toward the fence. Before we could react, he was yards ahead of us.

"Morgan! Stop!" Lucy cried. "Morgaaaan!"

We ran into the darkness with our flashlights lighting a narrow path ahead of us. We could hear Morgan running ahead of us. And then there was a crash and the sound of branches moving.

By the time we got to the fence, Morgan had slipped off into the trees. The fence was dilapidated and had plenty of openings for anyone to get through. Morgan had leapt right though one opening and past the warning signs. The skulls on the signs seemed to laugh at us in the beam of our flashlights, but the words were clear: "Explosives. Keep Out."

Lucy jumped through the opening Morgan had used. I stopped. "Wait!" I shouted. "You'll get killed."

Lucy answered just ahead of me in the trees, "Morgan weighs more than I do. I am going to step where he stepped. That voice must have been my grandfather's. Morgan seemed to think so."

I don't remember exactly what happened next. Flashlight beams bouncing up and down in the dark. Tree branches swinging in the night, showing where someone had gone before. The sound of branches snapping. Everyone breathing hard. I just kept focusing, listening, and quickly deciding where I placed each foot as I ran.

I could just make out in the darkness a structure, a building of sorts. Nothing like the windmill. It was small and looked as though it was made of brick. There seemed to be a light on inside, seeping out from around the edge of a door. The huge dog sniffed the bottom of the door. I heard the cry for help one more time as Lucy arrived and grabbed the door handle.

Inside was a mostly empty room. A table and some chairs. And an old man tied in the corner. The dog raced toward him—nearly knocking him over. A bare light bulb hung from the ceiling. Lucy and I followed Morgan over to the old man, but then I heard the most alarming sound.

Someone had just slammed the door shut behind us, and it sounded as though he or she was bolting it, locking it very tight.

Chapter Seven

Providing a Final Warning

Lucy pulled away the handkerchief that someone had tied around her grandfather's mouth and that now was only halfway covering his face. He was bound up with rope and had a gag in his mouth to make it difficult for him to speak or shout.

"Grandpa, are you all right?" she asked anxiously, while untying him.

"I'm not hurt," he replied. "I am just thirsty. I am sorry I got you mixed up in this. I was poking around here, and the folks who run this place got nervous. They are hiding something. So, the other day one of them just grabbed me. They have been arguing about what to do with me ever since, but no one has hurt me, except by tying me up and not letting me leave and all."

"What is it that they are hiding and what have you been looking for here?"

"I wasn't interested in this dangerous dump. I think my search was leading to Windmolen, the old windmill. These folks just watched me climbing around here in the woods and in my boat and saw me looking through binoculars from the water. They got nervous. I made them feel uncomfortable because I was always climbing around. I am so sorry you are stuck in this mess. And poor Morgan! How is my Morgan?"

Morgan leaned his huge weight into Lucy's grandfather while sitting right on the old man's feet. He pressed his head against the old man and looked for every chance to lick his hands and face. His tail thumped and generated a small breeze. Morgan could not be happier. To him everything was all right now because he was with Lucy's Grandpa. That's all he wanted.

I explained how I had found the map and, just tonight, crossed paths with Lucy at the windmill.

Lucy cut in with a question: "What is it you are looking for and what does it have to do with Windmolen?"

But before the old man could answer, the single light went out. And we could hear shouting in the distance. Morgan started to growl. "Morgan, quiet," said Lucy's grandfather. There was more shouting. And then what sounded like a gunshot. Morgan broke into a roar, barking loudly. "Morgan, quiet!" the old man yelled. "You'll get us all killed!" The dog stopped barking as if he understood. Perhaps he could sense the old man was very upset.

82

We listened in the darkness. The shouting grew louder or perhaps those doing the shouting were just getting closer. Then we heard the sound of someone fiddling with the door of the building we were in. Next, we heard a voice. "Drop it! This is your final warning!" someone shouted. Followed by the loudest sound of all: another gun shot rang out, right by the door.

We held our breath. Morgan whimpered into the old man's lap. The door began to creak open.

Crrrrrreaaaak. The door opened.

A beam of light—it might have been several lights—shined through the door and lit up the wall on the other side of the room we were in. We held still, not knowing what was going on or what to expect. A figure with a gun stepped into the beam of light and into the room. Someone followed behind with an electric lantern that lit up the room. Standing before us was the man with a gun. Next to him was, I was shocked to see, the fisherman who had given me a lift earlier that day.

"Willie!" I shouted. "What are you doing?! What's going on here?"

"Paul, it's me," said a familiar voice. The fisherman pulled off his hat and coat and, finally, a false beard. He stood up straighter and pushed his shoulders back.

There, before me, was Geo!

"I have been poking around this area dressed as 'Willie' the fisherman," Geo explained. "I put the costume back on—I had it in the car—in an effort not to alarm these folks when I came back with some of the plainclothes police. Since they had just chased us away with the truck earlier and probably thought they had killed us, I thought a costume would be in order."

It was amazing how Geo transformed himself with a simple costume and a change in posture. He also altered his voice a bit and turned himself into "Willie" the fisherman.

"And this is Sergeant MacDonald," Geo said.

The policeman nodded. "We had been watching this place for a while. Geo here really helped us put an end to the shenanigans they were up to. We just had to fire a warning shot and, of course, the other shot to break open the lock on this door."

"What were they up to? Selling old munitions?" I asked.

"There are no munitions," said the sergeant. "New, old, or otherwise! My men are chasing them down toward the beach now. They might be trying to make a break for it by boat," said the sergeant.

"Now?" I asked in alarm. "This is the wrong time for anyone to go out in a boat. A storm is brewing."

Lucy's grandfather nodded in agreement. "In my bones I could feel the air pressure dropping. I don't have to look outside to know it is going to be bad weather out there."

We headed outside. The wind was now joined by rain. Lucy, her grandfather, and Morgan went off toward the police cruiser. Geo and I hopped into Geo's car. We headed for Windmolen to see what was happening with the chase that likely now had moved onto the water out in the bay. As we approached, a flash of lightning lit up the windmill.

Out on the water a motorboat was struggling though the waves as it was lit up now and then by the lightning. The waves were so big the boat was just plodding along but was making modest headway. The bad guys seemed to be getting away as the police at the scene did not have a boat to use. The criminals seemed to be escaping to freedom, but then their engine gave out. Its whirr rising and falling in the wind was suddenly replaced by just the sounds of the storm. I will never forget what happened next. Everything was suddenly lit up like daytime as a jagged flash of lightning and boom of thunder exploded at the same time. It looked as though if it did not actually strike the three figures in the stranded motorboat, it must have struck right next to them. Just then a Coast Guard cutter approached. The criminals, if they were alive, had run out of luck.

And so began a long night of sorting out what had happened.

Chapter Eight

Two Surprises–Late in the Game

The next day the reporters gathered in the sun up by the old windmill. The storm had blown through, leaving a blue sky and gorgeous cumulonimbus clouds. Some of the news had made its way to the radio stations before morning, but there were still questions to ask and be answered about what happened and had been happening at the old munitions dump. Many left that press conference surprised.

Sergeant MacDonald first made a statement on behalf of the Southampton Town Police. He explained that unusual activity had raised concerns about what was going on at what we had all been calling the "old munitions dump," but some clever observations and research by Geo and work with the police had led to the conclusion that this had never been a munitions dump. The whole story had been made up by a syndicate of criminals. They came up with a plan by which they would drive down the price of prime real estate—right next to the bay and in the shadow of the historic windmill—by creating a false story.

They then put up the signs and created numerous accounts and references to the "old munitions dump" and seeded them on the Internet. A whole fake history, including fabricated wartime photos, was placed on various websites. Some photos were created just to make the entire rouse seem more real. This made-up history and all the fake photos then took on a life of their own. People believed it was a true history and started acting like it was. The whole scam reached a new level when, eight years ago, environmental groups referred to the fake dump, which they saw as an example of a toxic dump. It became a local cause for them, playing right into the hands of the swindlers.

These swindlers planned to approach the state with an offer to buy the land at a low price and clean it up. Of course, no cleaning would be needed. The same group now faced charges of kidnapping and attempted murder.

Geo took the podium next. He said there would be another announcement today related to the site. As part of his own investigation, countless days walking the beaches and woods, he had made another discovery: because so few people had been going past the fake warning signs in recent decades, at least two endangered species of bird had made their home here. This, combined with the excellent state of the water table below the land, so important to the area and life in the bay, has already convinced local and state authorities to preserve ninety-six acres in this area as a protected wildlife sanctuary and park for the windmill.

The press conference went on for an hour and a half, but those were the two headlines—the scam and the plans for a new wildlife sanctuary—you could read that week in the *Southampton Press* and various other newspapers. It was earth-shaking news for many.

The rapid chain of events had given us little time to process what was happening. Now, we finally could stop and take stock. For one, Geo and I got to know Lucy. She seemed almost scary when we thought she was following us with some evil intentions. She told us that she works as an elementary school history teacher in New Jersey. She lives alone but comes to visit her grandfather whenever she can. Summer gives her more chances to do this since she has some time off.

"It was my grandfather who inspired my interest in history," Lucy said. "He knew that if I saw that map you guys found on the beach, I would understand it right away: the references to William Merritt Chase and to Einstein and to the horseshoe crabs and to the glaciers. He told me about all of them countless times. Thanks to him I learned to look at the world around me very differently. Our history never goes away, does it? It shapes the world we live in today."

Lucy's grandfather nodded shyly in agreement.

"But why didn't you just tell her more details on the phone or leave the map in your house?" I asked.

"I had that 'map' as a back-up plan in case something happened to me. I hoped that Lucy would put the details together. She knew I was looking for something. I knew she was the only person likely to understand where that map was pointing. I kept it on my boat. I tossed it overboard in that bottle and in that box when I saw trouble coming. Those guys were following my boat one day and I thought they were up to something. I always used your house, Geo, as landmark when I was out in the bay. I happened to be near there when I tossed it. The storm brought it to your beach."

Talking further with her grandfather, we learned that he was retired and loves fishing. He also reminded us that he was looking for something. We still had one more mystery to solve: Windmolen's final secret.

Chapter Nine

A Flag on the Mill, a Ship in the Bay

After the press conference and after the reporters had all gone and the photographers had all taken their pictures, we all met as planned in the shadow of the windmill. We needed to hear again the story that Lucy's grandfather had told us the night before, once all the police reports had been filed. So, as agreed, we gathered: Lucy, her grandfather, Geo, Morgan, and I.

We made sure no one else was around, and then we began. Morgan, the giant dog, as I recall, was the least interested member of the group. He nodded off as Lucy's grandfather recounted the story. "Last summer my friend Cyril came over from England to visit. I thought he wanted to catch up on old times, but he had something he wanted to share. He told me how for generations a secret has been passed down to just a few people. It is believed to be the instructions for locating treasure that Captain Kidd buried in the late 1600s. For hundreds of years, those who heard the instructions thought they referred to places in England. After all, Kidd passed these instructions along just before he was executed in London about 1701. After generations of following the instructions, searching, and finding nothing, one day Cyril had an idea. Suppose the instructions don't refer to places in Europe but to places some-where else with similar names? Lucy's grandpa had a gleam in his eye as he told the story.

"So there was no map?" I asked. I had asked him this last night but needed to ask again as he retold the story.

"No map," he answered firmly. "As Cyril explained it, why would a pirate make a map and leave it behind? Anyone, friend or foe, can find the map and get right to the treasure. But if you pass along a secret by word of mouth, only your pals and ghosts will know. So, that's what Kidd did. For generations the verbal instructions have been passed along. Cyril told me the instructions, well just the few words that he knew, but he thought they were the key words. And then he up and died on me this past winter. God rest his soul."

The old man looked far across the bay, lost in thought, and then refocused his attention. He looked around carefully and then lowered his voice. "The words I heard from Cyril were

'The Windmolen sundial past Southampton.'

"That's it. That's all we have. Cyril thought the Southampton in the instructions was not Southampton, England but Southampton, Long Island. And although for ages folks who had heard this thought the 'windmolen' was in the Netherlands where they speak Dutch, we began to explore windmills in this area. We thought this very building held the best prospects."

He took a deep breath and went on: "So we searched inside here and all around. No treasure. No sundial. Cyril had to head back to England after a few weeks. I have been mulling it over for months but only ended up getting mixed up with the criminals next door who kidnapped me. Ha! To think, here I am looking for pirate treasure and get kidnapped—but not by pirates! Those dopes thought an old man like me was some sort of investigative reporter or something. What idiots!"

He lowered his voice again, "I called my granddaughter to come help me with this. I made that map you found hoping she would use it if something happened to me. I knew she would be able to figure it out. As she was growing up I would tell her the history of the area. I knew she would recognize those symbols. To think, I was making a pirate's treasure map in the twenty-first century! I had to throw the map overboard in a hurry when those thieves looked like they were chasing me one day. The box must have floated down the beach a ways. Thankfully, you all found each other and rescued me." The old man grew quiet.

Geo, who had been very quiet and listening, suddenly spoke up, "I would like to walk around here a bit. Are there any interesting markings on the old windmill?"

"Yes, take a look," said the old man. "But I don't think there is anything helpful."

"First, one weird thing is that, despite its name, this is not a Dutch-style windmill. It's an English-style windmill," said Geo. "Which makes sense when you consider that the English and not the Dutch had dominant influence on the East End during the colonial period, but it sure is strange."

"It would make sense if it's tied into the Captain Kidd legend as we heard from grandpa. You remember the clues that have been passed down verbally included the word *windmolen*," added Lucy. "That may have been a way to slightly disguise the fact that it was tied to a windmill. They may have picked the Dutch word so it would not be very obvious. Let's take a closer look."

We all walked slowly around the ancient structure, which rested on a stone foundation. Chiseled into the stone in different places were a few items that Geo looked very interested in. There was the date 1689 on one stone, but the most noticeable was an old and famous saying about the weather. It read,

St Swithun's day if thou dost rain
For forty days it will remain
St Swithun's day if thou be fair
For forty days 'twill rain na mair

"Interesting," said Geo. "That old poem." I just cannot remember when St. Swithun's day is!

"Oh, sure. I know that." I chimed in. "As a weatherman, that is something I learned. July fifteenth is St. Swithun's Day."

"Then forty days from St. Swithun's day would be August twenty-fourth. Fascinating," said Geo.

"What's that mean to you?" asked Lucy's grandpa. "Do you think Captain Kidd's ghost is going to show up on that day and hand you some jewels? Ha, ha, ha! That's the day after tomorrow!"

"I'm not sure yet," answered Geo, "but let's keep looking around."

"I'm going back inside the windmill," said Lucy. "I think it will be a more positive experience in the daytime!" She headed for the windmill's door and opened it with a loud creak and went in.

"Look at this, Morgan!" said the old man, "there's a little picture of a doggy here." Morgan dashed over just because he heard his name and leaned against the side of the old man and wagged his tail. Geo and I headed over to join them.

On another foundation stone was the faint outline of a dog and what looked like a bell shape. Just those two shapes were chiseled into the stone. Each about the same size. Side-by-side. "What do you make of that?" asked Lucy's grandfather.

"I'm not sure," said Geo. "A bell and a dog. Do they mean anything to you guys? Any connection with time? The St. Swithun's poem refers to dates."

"Time?" thought the old man. "Well, come to think of it, there is that old style way of referring to time according to bells on a ship. You know—'eight bells' and all of that."

95

"What would one bell mean?" I asked.

"One bell would be..." Lucy's grandpa paused. "Hey, I just thought of something. The evening watches—First Dog Watch and Second Dog Watch. First Dog Watch starts at four p.m. One bell would be four thirty p.m.!"

"We might be on to something," Geo said triumphantly.

Just then we heard Lucy's voice. "Come up here and check this out!"

Morgan waited at the bottom of the stairs as we made our way to the top of the windmill. The darkness seemed much less scary with other people around and knowing it was daylight outside. Step by step, the three of us climbed to the top into the little room on the top floor. Windows on two sides offered a dramatic view of the area. Lucy stood by the window facing east.

"Look down here," she said, pointing under a wooden bench built into the wall under the window. Geo raced over.

"Aha!" he exclaimed.

I was the next one to look under the bench. Just visible in the faint light were the words: "Cara Merchant." The letters were handwritten in ink and varnished into the wood. "Cara Merchant? What's that mean?" I asked.

"Cara Merchant!?" whispered Lucy's grandpa. "That's the name of one of Captain Kidd's last ships. The one that no one ever found. This is...! Could it be true?"

"Could what be true?" I asked

96

"That this windmill is made from the wood of Captain Kidd's ship!"

We were all in shock. To think, the famous lost ship of a notorious pirate was not buried somewhere. It was not resting at the bottom of the ocean. It was in plain sight for all to see but recycled, so to speak, as a windmill! There's no better way to hide treasure than by putting it in an obvious place that people can see for miles but where they don't expect it!

We spent the next half hour searching the inside of the windmill but found no more clues. We went to look around more outside. Morgan was very happy about this. He was happy to see us all again and marched around wagging his tail at the reunion. He was pleased when we started to stroll around the property, looking and looking. Morgan sniffed everywhere we went but, of course, did not know what we were looking for.

An hour passed. We were all hot from the sun. We decided to gather and think a little. And, frankly, we were all very tired.

"So what do we do next?" Lucy's grandpa asked. He was still in shock thinking about how the wood to make the windmill could be from Kidd's lost ship. "We have some dates and a time, perhaps, if those are clues. BUT we haven't found a sundial yet."

We were at a loss. Morgan walked over to where there was some shade so that he could lie down. He found a cool spot in the shadow of the tall windmill. Geo watched the huge dog settle down on the ground.

"A sundial! We DO have a sundial!" Geo announced proudly.

"Where?" I asked looking around the level area.

"Windmolen!" Geo answered. "It's one big sundial!"

Chapter Ten

The Pirates' Chest

Two days later we were back and full of anticipation but not knowing what we would find. We were at what we thought was the right location: Windmolen. And on the right date: the twenty-fourth of August, which was, luckily, a sunny day. We arrived over an hour early, about three o'clock. The night before Lucy pointed out that they did not have anything like daylight saving time in the late 1600s, so we needed to watch a range of times, at least from three o'clock on. Our plan was to mark where the shadow of Windmolen fell from about three to five o'clock and then weigh our options.

The weather was cooperating nicely. The air pressure had been rising steadily, meaning that a high pressure system was moving in, as I had hoped and expected. Days like this usually involve dark blue skies and, often in this area, a cool wind from the north that blows away the humidity. The nights under these conditions are usually clear.

It became apparent at three o'clock what path the shadow was following. It moved in a smooth arc across the grass and was headed straight for a group of rocks. Right away we suspected that was our target. We spent the afternoon watching the shadow and sitting and talking so as not to look suspicious. After all, there was little we could do during the day. Just think how it would look to have the heroes from a few days before running around with shovels at the new nature preserve and windmill park. No matter what we saw that afternoon, we would have to return at night.

Sure enough, the shadow lingered on the group of stones—one of them huge—during the target time. We enjoyed the rest of the afternoon there and even brought a picnic and had dinner. Conversation naturally turned to Captain Kidd and why he made the choices he did.

"Kidd thought he could make lots of money really fast," Lucy informed us. "He was living well in Manhattan but wanted to make even more. He was basically greedy, if you ask me. He left his family behind and found some people to back his voyage, including the King of England, but running a ship full of greedy sailors can be tricky. Each person signs up for the trip with the expectation that he will get rich quickly. When months go by at sea and they were not getting the chance to steal treasure—to steal it from ships belonging to England's enemies as a privateer would do—they started attacking almost any ship, enemy or not. They became pirates. Kidd and his crew had crossed a line."

"He was in a bind when he tried to return home to New York," Lucy's grandfather added. "The political situation in London had changed, and the bigwigs no longer wanted to be associated with privateers and pirates. Word got back to New York that Kidd had crossed a line and become a pirate. He faced the prospect of death by hanging."

Lucy nodded in agreement. "So Kidd sailed around Long Island and tried to negotiate with the authorities before pulling his ship back into New York. We know he buried treasure on Gardiners Island east of here. Some wonder if there is more."

Geo laughed. "Kidd's greed is not unlike that of the bad guys who tried to steal the land next to here by swindling the state, taking from all of us really."

We watched the sun set and went back to Geo's. Our plan was to return at midnight with shovels. Meanwhile, we were all deep in thought. This discussion about greed made us think about what we would do if we found something valuable, actual treasure.

A wind had picked up by ten o'clock, blowing from the north right off of Great Peconic Bay. It was so clear you could see the lights of houses across the bay toward the town of Mattituck. There were countless stars.

Geo and I carried the shovels. Lucy and her grandfather carried some old potato sacks. Morgan was thrilled to be in the night air and with the group. The big dog liked to be with his family, or to put it in dog terms with his "pack." He wagged his tail as we walked and tilted his nose in the air to smell the breeze over and over again.

We arrived at the group of rocks, which now were no longer just rocks in our minds but silent sentinels that had stood guard for centuries. Probably unnoticed by everyone— just a part of the landscape— they had a special aura that night. We paused briefly to note that they might not have been moved since they were placed here, perhaps by Captain Kidd himself.

We went right to work, silently digging. After about half an hour, Lucy's grandpa spoke up. "I don't know if you have heard about the curse of Captain Kidd's treasure."

"Curse?" Lucy asked excitedly.

"Yes, they say that to locate Captain Kidd's treasure three people need to gather with the moon over their shoulders and not make a sound as they dig up the treasure—or the treasure will disappear! Even if one person says, 'We found it!' Then, poof! All the treasure disappears! Just like that!"

"Why are you telling us this now?" I asked half joking.

"Because, I think it's a pile of nonsense! I like to see who gets scared by such stuff!" the old man laughed. Just then we heard a clang from Geo's shovel.

We held our breath. Lucy pointed her light into the hole we had dug. A dark metal strap was clearly visible, part of what looked like a wooden box. Geo used his shovel to clear away more of the dirt so we could see the outline of the box. It was huge and dark and musty with age. Geo hit the old lock with his shovel and slowly opened the top. We all held our breath. Suddenly, light from our flashlights glinted back at us from inside the chest off of countless coins—gold and silver—and was sent dancing in all directions.

Chapter Eleven

A New Wind

At first, we were thrilled to find real treasure. We ran our hands through the many coins and looked it all over, laughing and not believing our eyes. "Told ya!" I said to Geo in triumph. "It does not hurt to have a little imagination and to dream a little."

But then reality set in. Could we keep it? Would we want to keep it? After all, we dug it up off of public land. So who would be the owner? Would we be the owners because we found it? Or would the state of New York because it was found on the state's land?

"And to think of the people who were killed to get all this," Lucy added.

There were many coins in the treasure trove: English coins, Dutch coins, and some we are still trying to identify but that were probably Spanish coins. And there was endless gold jewelry: gold brooches with stylized animal shapes and eyes made of precious stones, necklaces of gold filigree, and dozens of small gold cases, some of which we have not been able to open. There were also countless gems. For me the stones that look like rubies are the most impressive. I am not sure whether I had ever actually held a ruby in my hand before; its dark red color has a regal and mysterious quality. Unfortunately, the color also reminds me of blood. And that brought us back to the question of what to do with all the precious items.

We got very quiet wondering about the many dramatic stories that likely lie behind each item. We stayed up almost all night thinking over the options. Slowly, the thought of trying to create a larger good of what started out as greed, death, and destruction became more and more attractive to us. Perhaps, in some small way, it could even help the ghost of Captain Kidd rest. He never made it back home and never had the chance to go back to his life in Manhattan. He was hanged in London for being a pirate. We thought of a plan to do something good for many people and at the same time develop fuller lives for ourselves.

That exciting night when we found the treasure was about a year ago. Since then Lucy has opened a museum that she set up with the state of New York in the shadow of the windmill to display many of the items we found. Her grandpa helps out and acts as a guide on boat tours around the windmill. Morgan is always at his side. I broadcast weather reports from a weather station near the old windmill in an interpretive center about the environment, the weather, and wind power. It's part of what has become the *Windmill by the Bay Foundation*. Geo is its director and biggest contributor.

Geo is for me one of the remaining mysteries. What motivated him to start this adventure in motion? What is it about his past that shaped his way of looking at the world? And what happened years ago that left him using a cane at times to walk? I'll have to save those answers for another time.

Geo added one more success to the story; he managed to get the windmill functioning again. He worked for months with several historians and carpenters to restore it properly. When the weather cooperates and the wind is just right, its sails bulge with unseen strength, and the whole windmill comes to life.

Not the end...

Learn About the History of Eastern Long Island

Although *Windmolen: The Secret of the Windmill by the Bay* is fiction, and there is no windmill on Long Island called "Windmolen," many of the historical references mentioned in this book are based on historical facts. For example, Captain Kidd did bury treasure on Gardiners Island, William Merritt Chase painted many paintings showing Shinnecock Hills and nearby beaches, Einstein did send a letter to President Roosevelt in 1939 about the atomic bomb, and he did sail in Little Peconic Bay. There are a number of historic windmills still standing on eastern Long Island for you to visit; they are treasures to preserve so that we all can enjoy them, and future generations can learn from them. Of course, you can discover more at your library.

Also, please visit WindmillByTheBay.com for links on the history of Long Island and for more about upcoming stories in this series. You'll even find links to reports on how the real *Cara Merchant* may have been discovered in the Caribbean and is being investigated by underwater archeologists from Indiana University.

WindmillByTheBay.com

Simon Finn

Eastern Long Island and the tales of Captain Kidd's treasure first captured Simon Finn's imagination when he spent summers in the Shinnecock Hills area as a child. Simon never found any treasure, so he says, but he probably wouldn't tell us if he had. He now lives in Virginia but enjoys returning to Long Island to visit family members and to kayak around the bays and ponds of the East End.

Simon claims to have graduated from Georgetown University and the University of Cambridge, but not many people have actually asked for evidence of this. He currently poses as an international affairs and media analyst when not writing fiction or messing around in boats.

Windmolen: The Secret of the Windmill by the Bay is the first of a series of books involving Geo, Lucy, and Paul. Please visit WindmillByTheBay.com for information about the next book, updates, and excuses or to offer praise, complaints, or personal secrets.

Find the clues...

The title of the next book in this series is hidden in this book. Perhaps you can spot the pattern and find the answer?

Please visit WindmillByTheBay.com for more information.